Here and There

Kane Miller

A DIVISION OF EDC PUBLISHING

First American Edition 2018
Kane Miller, A Division of EDC Publishing

Conceived by Weldon Owen, An Imprint of Kings Road Publishing

Copyright © 2018 Weldon Owen, An Imprint of Kings Road Publishing

Illustrated by Greg Paprocki
Written by Susie Rae

For information, contact:
Kane Miller, A Division of EDC Publishing
PO Box 470663
Tulsa, OK 74147-0663

www.kanemiller.com
www.edcpub.com
www.usbornebooksandmore.com

Library of Congress Control Number: 2017942265

Printed in China
3 4 5 6 7 8 9 10

ISBN: 978-1-61067-714-1

Contents

Here and There...
Introduction

Have you ever wondered how people travel around the crowded cities of Vietnam? Or how they celebrate the New Year in Colombia? How about what people eat for lunch in France? Get ready to experience the incredible diversity of our planet's people, countries, and cultures in amazing technicolor. Take a journey through the rain forests of Borneo, join a game of soccer on the street in Brazil, experience the lights and colors of Iran's Festival of Fire, and so much more.

There are almost 200 countries on Earth, with seven and a half billion people living in them. This makes for thousands of different, exciting cultures. Every day, all around the world, people go about their lives in many curious and interesting ways. Doing chores, traveling to school, shopping for groceries, and even just enjoying the view from your bedroom window can be a very different experience depending on where in the world you are.

It is these little differences that make our planet so amazing. The incredible diversity of all the people around the world means that you will never run out of exciting new things to experience and fascinating people to meet. Can you imagine how boring life would be if everyone was the same?

So get ready to travel around the world, experiencing all the sights, sounds, smells, and tastes that our fantastic, diverse world has to offer. . . *Here and There*!

Buying Groceries

No matter where in the world you live, you need to eat! While some people can just walk down the street to the grocery store, or even order their groceries on the Internet, other people might shop at huge markets, or even grow food for themselves, their family, and their neighbors. In many countries, buying groceries is much more than a mundane chore—it can be an exciting experience, filled with interesting sights, tastes, and smells. Around the world, food markets are buzzing with people, and even attract tourists who love to look at the different stalls and sample interesting foods they can't get at home.

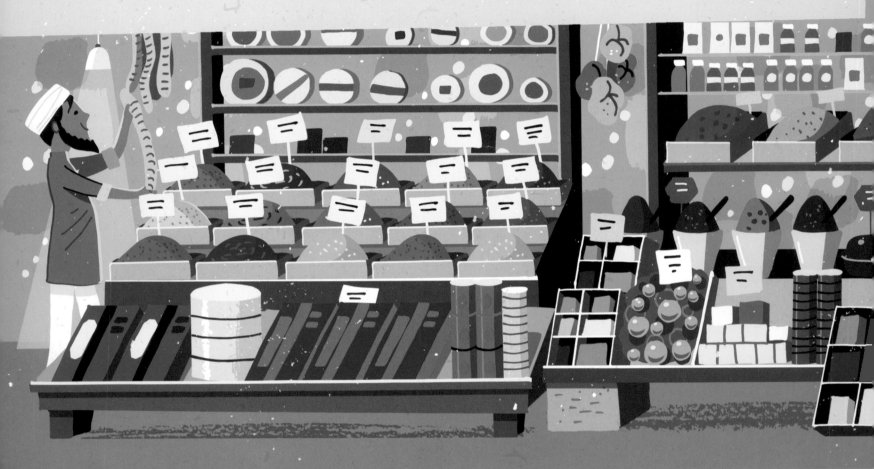

Bazaar flavors

In the Middle East, there are huge community markets called *bazaars*. People visit these bazaars to buy a vast range of things, but especially food and clothes. The biggest and most famous bazaars are the *Grand Bazaar* and the *Egyptian Bazaar* in Istanbul, Turkey. The Grand Bazaar is enormous, with sixty-one streets and over 4,000 stalls. Some of the most exciting things you can find at these bazaars are stalls filled with huge bags of interesting-smelling spices.

Going to market

All around the world, from Seattle to Bangkok to Istanbul, people visit markets to buy their groceries. Vendors set up beautiful stalls, selling all sorts of different things, and customers move from stall to stall, buying everything they need. Fruit, meat, flowers, clothes, rugs, spices. . . you can find almost anything in the world's markets. In Barcelona, Spain, *La Boqueria* sells fresh local food, or you can visit *Chatuchak Weekend Market* in Bangkok, Thailand, to buy delicious Thai food, bright clothing, and even furniture.

What's in store?

In many countries, especially in Europe and North America, most people buy their groceries from grocery stores. Here, you can find almost any food under one roof. There are lots of choices, and food is sold in brightly colored packaging to make it stand out and look appealing. Nowadays, many people don't even leave the house to buy their groceries—they can order them online and have them delivered to their door.

On the road

In many remote areas of the world, there are sometimes no grocery stores or markets at all. In parts of Peru, and other South American countries, farmers travel around with carts, selling food they have grown or made. Often, these food carts only visit an area once a week, or even once every few weeks, so people need to plan everything they will need in advance. Many people in rural areas around the world grow their own food, or raise animals for food and milk.

Grocery shopping in...
North America

One of the ways that people in North America can shop for food is by going to a supermarket. These huge stores have almost every kind of food you can think of, from fresh fruit and vegetables to precooked meals.

People pick up the things that they want and carry them around in a basket or push them in a shopping cart.

Freezers and refrigerators keep meat, dairy, and other foods fresh.

Big supermarkets sell lots of other things besides food. They also sell household items, magazines, and sometimes even books and technology.

When customers have chosen everything they need from the store, they pay for their items at a cash register.

The floating markets of Indonesia, Thailand, and Vietnam are popular tourist attractions.

Grocery shopping in...

Indonesia

In Indonesia, there are floating markets on the rivers. People sell flowers, fruit, and vegetables that they have grown, and food that they have made.

At the floating markets, people buy, sell, or barter for everything they need.

The smaller boats sometimes form a line and hitch a ride to the market tied to the back of larger boats!

Playing Outdoors

Children all over the world love playing outdoors. Whether in a city or the country, there are lots of opportunities to run around in the fresh air. Many places will have special outdoor spaces, but in other areas children may have to make their own playground. Playing outside can be very different depending on where you live—the games you can play in very hot places are different from the activities available in snowy countries—but you can have a lot of fun no matter where you are.

Hot stuff

In hot countries, there are plenty of opportunities to play outdoors, but it is important to stay safe in the sun. In Mexico, many children play games like soccer on the beach, where they can swim in the sea to cool down. Other hot countries, like Indonesia and the United Arab Emirates, have huge water parks where people can cool down and have fun at the same time.

Keeping it cool

In Canada, it is very cold during the winter—but that doesn't stop people from playing outdoors. Ice hockey is a very popular game, and children and adults play it on frozen lakes and ponds.
Children in Finland and Sweden are also used to snowy conditions, and many learn to ski at a young age.

Going green

Almost every single country in the world has parks—wide, green, public spaces for people to enjoy. Nearly half of Edinburgh, in Scotland, is made up of parks, and people go there to skateboard, play tennis, and be in the outdoor space with their friends. Central Park in New York City is two and a half miles long, and has a huge lake, spaces to play sports, and even its own zoo.

Close to home

The easiest place to play is often your own neighborhood. In Brazil, children can be seen playing soccer out in the streets, and children in the Netherlands ride their bikes and play in the neighborhood with their friends. Many homes in Australia, the US and the UK have their own backyards, where children can explore nature and play outdoors in a safe environment.

Class act

Playing outdoors isn't just fun—it's also educational. Most schools give children a chance to play outdoors during the school day, and more and more schools are making it a part of classes. There are even schools in Scandinavian countries like Sweden which are now mostly outdoors. These outdoor schools are called *udeskole*. Rural schools in New Zealand are also commonly outdoors, particularly in Maori communities.

Playing outdoors in...
Norway

Playing outdoors is a very important part of life in Norway, and children spend a lot of their day outside, even when they're at school. It is often very cold, especially in the winter, but this doesn't stop them from wrapping up warm and playing in the snow.

There are lots of mountains in Norway, so skiing and snowboarding are popular activities.

At *udeskole*, almost all classes are held outdoors.

Most children learn to ski from a young age. This helps them get around in snowy winter conditions.

Some playgrounds are outdoors, but others are in large, indoor spaces.

Hong Kong

Hong Kong is a huge city, filled with people, buildings, and cars, so there isn't a lot of outdoor space. Most children play in specially built playgrounds with swings and jungle gyms.

Some local playgrounds are tiny, while others are huge, spread out over several levels.

Playgrounds can be found in nooks and crannies all around the city. There are some in parking lots, and inside apartment buildings. There's even one in an old castle!

Traveling to School

Getting to school every day is not always easy. Some children are lucky enough to live only a short walk or bus ride away from school, but many others live several miles away from the nearest school, and have to travel great distances just to get to class. Some children go to boarding school, where they live in the school, or in a nearby building, and only travel home for holidays. All over the world, children use some very interesting modes of transportation to get to class.

Wild journeys

The most remote school in the world is in the village of Gulu, China, and can only be reached after a five-hour trek through the Himalayas! Children in Riau, Indonesia, travel to school in canoes, while in rural parts of India, schools can be many miles apart, and children may get there in a horse and cart.

On your bike!

In many parts of France and the Netherlands, children travel to school together on a bike bus. These clever vehicles have a grown-up to steer, and all the passengers have their own set of pedals, like bike pedals, which make the bus move. Staying healthy is very important in the Netherlands, and this is a good way of keeping fit, as well as being much better for the environment than a bus or car.

High in the sky

In Caracas, Venezuela, some children get to school using cable cars, high above the city, to avoid having to walk or take the bus through dangerous neighborhoods. Not only do the cable cars help to keep them safe, they are also an exciting way to travel, offering a fantastic view of the whole city.

Buses, trains, and more

A common way of getting to school is by public transportation. In North America, many children travel in bright-yellow school buses. Other children might get driven to school by their parents, or carpool with friends or neighbors.

Count your footsteps

Lots of children around the world walk to school. In Ghana, many children have to walk several miles across hot desert to get to class. Children in the UK are helped on their walk to school by grown-ups known as lollipop men or women, who stand in the middle of busy roads holding a big sign that looks like a lollipop in order to stop traffic so the children can cross safely.

Traveling to school in...
Zambia

A lot of children in rural parts of Africa have to walk for up to three hours to get to and from school because there aren't that many schools around. They walk through bush, crossing elephant paths and rivers.

A lot of younger children are not able to go to school until they can walk the several miles a day needed to get there.

Some children take several trains to get to their school, commuting along with adults.

In Japan, children know that they can rely on help from the community if they need it.

A lot of Japanese schools require a uniform to be worn from the age of twelve.

Sometimes the nearest school can be up to six miles away.

They set out very early in the morning, before it is too hot, even if this means they arrive hours before school starts.

Traveling to school in...
Japan

Children in Japan usually travel to school alone from the age of six. Some walk, and some of them take the train. Children in Japan are taught to be independent from a young age.

Healthy Eating

It is very important to make sure you're eating the right types of food in order to maintain a healthy diet. Food is divided into four major groups: carbohydrates, protein, fruit and vegetables, and fats. People need to eat from all of these food groups to stay healthy.

The kinds of foods that people eat are different in different countries. People in urban communities in the US, Australia, and Canada tend to eat more processed and sugary foods, while people in rural communities in Asia, Africa, and South America tend to eat more fresh foods.

Carbohydrates

Healthy carbohydrates are in foods like fruit, beans, pasta, potatoes, and whole grains. It is very important to eat enough healthy carbohydrates to give you energy. In Japan, people eat around five to seven servings of carbohydrates a day, while in Caribbean countries like Haiti, people eat fewer carbohydrates.

Fruit and vegetables

Around the world, everyone agrees that eating fruit and vegetables is very important. They are a good source of vitamins and other vital nutrients. Many countries, including France, Germany, and Japan, recommend eating around five servings of fruit and vegetables a day. In rural areas, where people grow their own food, they tend to eat far more fruit and vegetables than people in urban areas.

Protein

Protein is necessary for muscle and bone growth. Meat, fish, eggs, and nuts are good sources of protein. People in the US and Australia eat the most protein, especially meat, while people in India and Bangladesh eat the least. In Tanzania and Zambia, people get the majority of their protein from fish, nuts, and seeds.

Fats

Most countries recommend limiting fat, but it is important to have some, as it helps the body store energy. Healthy fats can be found in foods like olive oil, nuts, avocado, and fish, as well as small amounts of milk, cheese, and sweets. In China and some other Asian countries, people eat very little milk and cheese.

Carbohydrates

Protein

Fruit and vegetables

Fats

17

School Lunches
Around the World

What kind of school lunch do you have? In South Africa, school commonly finishes at lunchtime, so children eat lunch at home, but in most other countries, school lunchtime is a staple of the day.

If you are lucky enough to live in Colombia, Scotland, or Sweden, the government provides school lunches for all or most children, while in many other countries children must bring or buy their own lunch.

Canada

Children in Canada can bring their own lunch to school. Their lunch bag might contain a sandwich, a juice box, and a snack like fruit or chips.

United Kingdom

In the UK, school lunches usually consist of meat and vegetables along with milk, juice, or water to drink. Many lunches also have a choice of hot dessert, fruit, or yogurt.

Finland

School lunches in Finland are usually very nutritious, made up of a choice of hot food, a side of vegetables, bread, milk, and water.

South Korea

It is normal for teachers and children in South Korea to eat the same lunch. Meals normally contain rice and soup, and a few side dishes, called *banchan*, such as *kimchi*, seaweed, fruit, or mixed vegetables.

South Africa

Schools in South Africa normally finish at lunch time, so school lunch isn't served. Instead, children go home for lunch, or buy food from street vendors outside the school.

Thailand

Before you can eat in a Thai school, you must *wai*—clasping your hands and bowing your head to say thank you. Lunches contain steamed rice and soup with vegetables, with a side of fruit and milk or water.

France

In France, school lunches can be three or even four courses! They are normally very healthy, with a mix of protein, vegetables, and a side of bread and butter.

India

School lunches are free for all children in India. Each child will get curry with a side of naan (Indian bread) and vegetables, and a local grain, in order to support local customs and communities.

Brazil

Most of the food in Brazilian school lunches is sourced from local farms. Some schools even have their own farms, with children helping to grow the fruit and vegetables they will have for lunch.

Singapore

Children in Singapore get lots of choices when it comes to lunch. Many school cafeterias are set up like a food court, with different kinds of food offered.

Chores

From cooking, cleaning, shopping for food, and collecting water, to looking after younger brothers and sisters, there are all sorts of chores that need to be done in any home. In most countries, everyone in a household is expected to do their part, and around the world, children help in all sorts of different ways. Some children get an allowance for doing chores, while others live in a culture where it is considered their responsibility.

Generational differences

For Chinese children, chores are considered a form of mental and physical exercise. In recent years, however, many Chinese families have started to view schoolwork as more important, and children are focusing more of their time on homework. This means that they help around the house less than their parents and grandparents did at their age.

Free time

Children in the UK help with chores less than many other children in the world. This is because many UK parents believe that children should have free time to relax, play, and socialize.

The gender gap

In most countries, girls end up doing far more around the house than boys! In fact, around the world, girls are thought to do forty percent more chores than boys. In India, most girls are expected to help their mothers around the house, while boys go to work at a young age to help earn money for the family.

Teamwork

Children in Japan are expected to do their share of chores not only around the house, but at school, too. In fact, most Japanese schools don't have custodians, and instead the children work together to keep the classrooms and corridors clean and tidy.

It's the law!

In Spain, it's not just good manners to help around the house—it's the law! The Spanish government passed a law in 2014 requiring children to do their homework, help with chores, and respect their parents. And this isn't just expected from children—Spanish marriage contracts state that both partners in a marriage have to do an equal share of work around the house!

Full-time job

Housework is so important in some countries that children, especially girls, will often miss school to do it. In Kenya, helping with chores—including fetching water, cleaning the house, cooking, and looking after younger brothers and sisters—can take children over six hours a day.

Doing chores in...
Belgium

In most Belgian families, both parents work outside the home, so children are expected to help out with chores around the house after school.

Many children get an allowance from their parents in exchange for doing chores.

Chores for children might include helping to cook, washing dishes after meals, keeping their bedrooms clean and tidy, and looking after pets.

Traditionally, most girls didn't go to school at all, but stayed at home to help their mothers look after the family. Nowadays, though, more and more girls are attending school and getting an education of their own.

Children in Uganda are expected to help their parents from a young age. They help to cook, clean, and look after younger children at home, and are also responsible for keeping their classroom clean if they go to school.

One important chore is collecting water. Some children walk up to four miles every day to get water.

Some children wake up early so they can do chores before they go to school.

New Year

New Year is a huge celebration around the world. It symbolizes a new start, leaving behind any bad luck in the old year, and hoping for good fortune in the year to come. Many people make New Year's resolutions, where they make a promise to change things in the new year. It is common to stay up late the night before, to celebrate when the clock strikes midnight.

In most countries, New Year happens on January 1. In China, Thailand, and several other countries in Asia, however, they use a different calendar. In these countries, New Year is celebrated at different times every year, depending on the cycles of the moon. This is called Lunar New Year.

Tasty tradition

In Spain and Argentina, people celebrate the arrival of the New Year by eating twelve grapes at the stroke of midnight. This symbolizes twelve months of good luck. Some people will try to eat all twelve before the clock has finished striking!

A smashing good time

People in Denmark bring their friends good luck by smashing plates against their front door. The more broken china you find outside your door on January 1, the more good luck you will have.

Starting with a bang

Lots of people set off fireworks to celebrate the arrival of the New Year. This tradition started in China, where people believed that loud noises would scare away evil spirits.

Having a wild time

People in some countries dress up as animals to scare away bad luck. In Romania, people dress up as bears and go door to door, singing and dancing. Many Asian communities, including in China, Vietnam, and Japan, have parades with huge, colorful dragon and lion puppets.

Giving thanks

In Nigeria, New Year is a religious time of year, and many people go to churches and mosques to pray and give thanks for the past year.

Making a splash

On the first day of the year, people across Europe run into lakes and rivers and swim in the cold water. This is most popular in the UK, but happens in Poland, Austria, the Netherlands, and Hungary, too.

New Year in...
China

People throw huge parades in the street to celebrate Lunar New Year. Large, colorful dragon and lion puppets perform dances to bring good luck to the community.

People set off firecrackers and wear red clothes, which ancient people believed would scare away evil spirits.

Adults often give children money in red envelopes called *lai see*.

New Year in...
Colombia

People throw big parties in the streets to celebrate New Year. An effigy, meant to represent the old year, is burned as the clock strikes midnight, and people throw pieces of paper with their faults, worries or mistakes written on them into the fire.

Running around the house or streets with a suitcase is said to guarantee travel in the New Year.

Wearing yellow clothes, especially underwear, at New Year is supposed to bring wealth.

New Year in...
Thailand

Thai New Year, or *Songkran*, marks the arrival of spring. This is celebrated with a water festival, where people splash water on each other, as a way of washing away any bad luck from the old year.

Rubbing chalk on the face is a way of blessing someone in Buddhist culture.

There are big water fights in the street, with fire trucks—and elephants—soaking people.

It is considered good luck to kiss the person you love at the stroke of midnight.

New Year in...
the United States

The biggest New Year celebration in the US happens in Times Square, in New York City. Thousands of people gather to celebrate. As the clock strikes twelve, a huge ball drops to the bottom of a flagpole to signal the start of the New Year.

Exercising

Exercise is very important for everyone. Combined with a balanced diet, it is the best way of keeping your mind happy and your body healthy. For millions of years, people have used different types of exercise to stay fit. Around the world, there are hundreds of fun and interesting sports and other exercises to try. Some types of exercise, like running, are *cardiovascular*—to keep your heart and lungs healthy—while others focus on strengthening your muscles. It is good to try a combination of both, but whatever you prefer, somewhere in the world you will find the right exercise for you!

Stretch it out

For thousands of years, people in India have been practicing yoga. Yoga is a form of exercise where you hold your body in different positions, in order to build strength and flexibility and focus your mind. Yoga is now popular all over the world, with millions of people practicing it every day.

Fighting fit

Across Asia, people have practiced martial arts for thousands of years. In Japan, judo, aikido, and sumo wrestling are very popular, while taekwondo is practiced in Korea, and muay Thai in Thailand. Martial arts are also practiced in other parts of the world. In Brazil, many people enjoy capoeira, a graceful and powerful combination of fighting and dance.

A healthy culture

In Japan and China, radio stations play a fifteen-minute exercise program in the morning, and most companies and schools do mandatory exercise every day. Even elderly people take exercise very seriously, and you can see dozens of elderly people practicing tai chi, another martial art, in parks across China and Japan.

Weird and wonderful

Some people exercise in unusual ways. In France, parkour, in which people create an outdoor obstacle course from walls, benches, and anything else they can find, has become popular. A tradition in Catalonia, Spain, involves building a huge human pyramid called a *castell*, which can involve up to 500 people. A different exercise trend in the US is roller derby, where teams race each other around a circuit on roller skates.

On the run

One of the easiest ways to exercise is to go running, as no equipment is needed, and it can be done almost anywhere. Main roads in Colombia are closed every Sunday so people can go running safely. In Kenya, running is taken very seriously—and it shows! Many of the greatest marathon runners in the world are Kenyan. Here, children start running at an early age, often running several miles to and from school every day.

Exercising in...
Australia

The weather in Australia is almost always warm and sunny, so there are lots of opportunities to exercise outside. Tennis, cricket, and golf are all popular sports. Australia has hundreds of beautiful beaches, which are the perfect place to get out and exercise in the sunshine.

Beach volleyball can be set up easily and played with as few as two players—and it's a lot of fun!

With its beautiful ocean and big waves, Australia is one of the best places in the world to go surfing.

The most popular sports in Australia are cricket and Australian Rules football, which is similar to American football. It is played on an oval field.

Exercising in...
Brazil

People in Brazil are crazy about soccer! Children and adults alike will play it almost anywhere—in the country, on the beach... or even on the street. Children in cities will gather in alleys and streets to play soccer with their friends.

The time spent playing street soccer definitely pays off—Brazil has one of the best soccer teams in the world.

If there are no goalposts, shirts, water bottles, or even piles of garbage can be used to mark the goals.

Nothing stands in the way of a game of soccer—if you don't have soccer cleats, just play barefoot! If there's no ball, a drink can or bottle will do.

Nature

Anywhere you go on Earth, you will find incredible plants, animals, and habitats. From hot, dry deserts, to freezing mountaintops, nature is amazing and diverse. Every country has its own plant and animal life, and there is nothing quite as mind-blowing as seeing a wild animal in its natural habitat. It's up to us to look after our planet and keep it safe.

Sea la vie

Because they are surrounded by water and isolated from the rest of the world, islands are often home to unique wildlife. Madagascar has flat-tailed geckos, which can disguise themselves as almost anything on the forest floor, and fierce, catlike predators called fossa. On the Galapagos Islands, near Ecuador, you might be lucky enough to spot a Galapagos giant tortoise, which can grow over four feet long and live up to 150 years!

Snowy peaks

There are mountains on every single continent. These wonders of nature can be very cold, but that doesn't stop some hardy animals from making a home there! Mountain goats, for example, are incredibly sure-footed, and can clamber up steep cliff faces. Rodents called marmots live high up in the Alps, in Europe, and survive in the freezing conditions by storing lots of extra fat in their bodies to keep them warm.

Green grass

Grasslands are too dry for many trees to grow, but there is enough rain to produce lots of grass. They have lots of different names—savannahs in Africa, prairies in North America, and pampas in South America. A massive twenty-five percent of our planet's land is grassland. The Serengeti, in Tanzania and Kenya, is home to some of the world's most amazing wildlife, including lions, giraffes, African elephants, and wildebeest.

City critters

It's not just humans who live in towns and cities. Around the world, animals live in urban habitats, eating food that human beings have thrown away. In Nara, Japan, more than 1,000 sika deer roam the streets, and in South Africa, people live alongside baboons. There have even been sightings of leopards living in cities in Nairobi and Kenya.

In the jungle

These incredible habitats are very hot and wet. There is over 100 inches of rain per year in most rain forests, and the air is always humid and damp. This amount of water makes it easy for plants to grow, which means there is plenty for animals to eat. Around half of all the plant and animal species in the world live in rain forests. The biggest rain forest is the Amazon rain forest in South America, which spreads out over nine countries and is home to many amazing creatures including sloths, anacondas, and macaws.

Deserted lands

Deserts are the driest places in the world, with less than ten inches of rainfall a year. Though most deserts are very hot, some can be freezing cold—the largest desert on the planet is Antarctica! The largest *hot* desert is the Sahara, which spreads over ten African countries. Conditions are very tough, and the animals that make their home there survive on very little water.

Nature in...
Borneo

Most of Borneo is covered with lush rain forest, filled with hundreds of different birds and animals, and thousands of amazing plants.

Rain forests are disappearing, but many people are fighting to protect these important habitats.

Borneo is home to the orangutan—a beautiful, endangered ape known for its bright-orange fur.

Nature in...
Morocco

The southern part of Morocco is dominated by the Sahara Desert. Though it may be sweltering hot, plenty of animals, and even people, make their home here.

The Tuareg people live in the Sahara Desert in parts of North and West Africa, and are experts in desert survival.

Desert animals have adapted to live in this hot, dry habitat. Lizards called thorny devils can drink water collected on their skin.

Nature in...
Canada

The Rocky Mountains—one of the most spectacular mountain ranges in the world—stretch from Canada to New Mexico, and are home to some incredible wildlife.

The Rockies have plenty of fresh water and food to eat, making them the perfect habitat for many animals.

The huge moose is native to Canada. It can be taller than an adult man.

Nature in...
Peru

Peru is home to some huge, sprawling grasslands called puna. Many people use this fertile land to grow crops and raise animals.

Puna are at risk of disappearing; the soil has been damaged by farming, and the use of fire to clear large areas.

Festivals

There are hundreds of different festivals all around the world. Some are somber events, while others are bursting with color, light, and noise. Many festivals are huge community celebrations, with parades and parties, while others are an opportunity to spend time with loved ones. Festivals take place for a variety of reasons: some are religious events, some celebrate the beginning of a new year or the start of spring, and others remember specific events in a country's history. Nowadays, many festivals attract tourists who want to experience the sights, sounds, and tastes of different countries at their most vibrant.

Let's give thanks

In some parts of North America, particularly in the US and Canada, Thanksgiving is an opportunity to give thanks for all the good things in your life. Thanksgiving was traditionally a celebration of a good harvest, so food is an important component.

A sacred feast

Passover is a Jewish festival that commemorates the exodus from Egypt. In Israel, the celebrations last for two weeks, and start with a big meal called the *Seder*, where people sing songs, pray, and tell the Passover story.

Day of the Dead

Día de Muertos is a Mexican festival; it offers a chance for people to honor friends and family who have died. The celebration actually lasts for three days—the first day remembers dead children, the second remembers adults and the third remembers all souls. People decorate the graves of loved ones with flowers, colored paper, and food. There are big parades where people paint their faces, and exchange gifts including chocolate and brightly colored sugar skulls.

Let there be light

Diwali, the Hindu festival of lights, is celebrated across many countries, including India, Nepal, and Fiji. The celebrations last for five days, around the darkest night of the year. People wear new clothes and light candles and lanterns to symbolize the triumph of light over darkness. Fireworks are set off, and people exchange gifts.

Flower power

In the spring, people in the Netherlands celebrate with a tulip festival, where they admire the beautiful, colorful flowers.

Blossoming into spring

In Japan, many people celebrate spring by having *hanami* picnics underneath cherry trees, filled with pink blossoms.

People dress in bright colors and have huge celebrations on the street where they throw colorful paint powder at each other.

A festival in...
India

Holi, or the Festival of Colors, marks the beginning of spring in India. It celebrates the triumph of good over evil and is a day to play, have fun and spend time with friends.

A festival in...
Italy

One of the most important holidays in Italy is Christmas, the Christian celebration of the birth of Jesus. Celebrations last for almost a month, and people go to church, sing carols and exchange gifts with their families.

Many homes will have a small nativity scene, which tells the story of the birth of Jesus. The baby Jesus is added to the scene on Christmas Eve.

A festival in...
Burma

Thadingyut, the Burmese Festival of Lights, marks the end of the rainy season. It begins the day before the full moon, and lasts for three days, with big celebrations in the streets.

Fireworks and hot air balloons lit with candles are sent skyward.

It is a time to give thanks to parents and teachers.

A festival in...
Iran

The Festival of Fire in Iran is held on the last Wednesday before New Year. Its full name is *Chaharshanbe Suri*, but it is sometimes called Red Wednesday. The color red symbolizes good health.

Fireworks are set off and lanterns are released into the sky.

People have celebrations where they jump over bonfires. This is meant to cleanse them of any sickness or sadness from the past year.

Getting Around

Most people travel around their town, city, or country by walking or driving, but there are so many other ways of getting around. The best way will be very different depending on where you are. If you are in a city, you might need to find a way to avoid busy roads and traffic. People in areas with lots of mountains might need to navigate steep, bumpy roads, or even no roads at all.

Training wheels

Most cities have buses, trains, or trams, which are a cheap and easy way of getting around. London, UK, is known for its bright-red, double-decker buses. Some cities, including Chicago, Cape Town, and Beijing, have underground train systems that transport people under the city.

Snow business

Snowy weather can make it much harder to travel, as roads become too slippery for cars or buses. People who live in cold countries have had to come up with some very clever ways of getting around.

In Siberia, Russia, many people travel the vast, snowy landscape on sleds pulled by specially trained dogs. Sled dogs have even been used in the past to deliver mail in parts of Canada, and Alaska.

In Minnesota, some children ride snowmobiles to get to school, while children in Norway might ski to class.

On a roll

In many parts of Asia, including Vietnam and Pakistan, people travel around in vehicles called *rickshaws*—a bicycle with a cabin attached for people to ride in. Rickshaws are smaller than cars, making it easier to navigate the narrow, winding streets of cities. In Thailand, people ride motorized vehicles, like a mix between a rickshaw and a car, called *tuk-tuks*.

Ferried around

To avoid busy roads, you could try traveling by water. Towns and cities by the sea, or on rivers, often have public boats called *ferries* that people use to get around. In Greece, there are lots of little islands, and people use ferries to travel between them. The city of Venice, in Italy, has no roads at all, and instead has a complex network of canals.
People can travel these watery streets in long, flat boats called *gondolas*, propelled by a *gondolier*.

Getting around...
Vietnam

The cities in Vietnam can be quite crowded, and the streets are narrow, so the easiest way to get around is by bike. Motorcycles, bicycles, rickshaws, and bike taxis fill the roads as people travel to and from work and school, run errands and visit different parts of the city.

A *xe om* is a motorbike taxi. For a fee, you can ride on the back of the motorbike, and the driver will take you wherever you need to go.

Bikes are an eco-friendly mode of transportation and help reduce air pollution.

Bicycle rickshaws called *cyclos* are a common way of transporting several people at once. In the old days, these were pulled by hand.

Some "scenic route" trains purposely travel through beautiful parts of the German countryside.

Getting around...
Germany

Germany is a very easy country to travel around, as it is networked by high-speed trains. These trains connect the major cities, but also towns and neighborhoods. Thousands of people take the train every day to travel around Germany.

The trains have comfortable seats, and some even serve food on board.

Trains can be caught at stations around the country. Bigger stations have dozens of trains arriving and leaving at once.

23

Through a Window

No two views from any window are exactly the same. Every window in the world shows a unique view of a city, town, village, or countryside. Some windows are high up in skyscrapers, looking out over the city skyline, while other windows may give a view of a sprawling, green landscape. Many windows look out onto the streets of a town or city, giving a view of the hustle and bustle of daily life in the neighborhood.

In the backyard

The UK does not have a very large population, so in many towns and villages nearly every house has its own backyard. This can offer a very peaceful view, looking out at a little slice of home.

City slickers

Hong Kong is a huge city with more skyscrapers than anywhere else in the world. Windows high up in these towering buildings look out over the dazzling skyline, with hundreds of skyscrapers surrounding a huge harbor. Other cities with amazing skyscraper views include Shanghai in China, and Dubai in the United Arab Emirates. The *Burj Khalifa*, the tallest building in the world, is in Dubai.

Raising the roof

If you live in Egypt, you might have a view across your city's rooftops. The roofs of most buildings in Egypt are flat, and people use them for hanging laundry, or as a space to relax in the sun. Many people even grow lush urban gardens on their rooftops, creating an incredible view across the top of the city.

Looking back at you

Living in a busy city, packed with buildings, means that your window may look out onto more windows! Manila, in the Philippines, has more people per square mile than anywhere else in the world, so the buildings are very close together. A view from a window in Manila might look out into an office building, buzzing with people going about their day, or it might look into a residential building, with dozens of different homes.

Looking through a window in...
Bangladesh

Most Bangladeshi farmers are men.

The Ganges River flows through Bangladesh, making the land perfect for growing crops and raising animals. Most of Bangladesh is countryside, filled with farms and small village communities. The landscape is very green, covered with beautiful trees.

Many people use the river for fishing. Others fill boats with fruit and vegetables and sail up the river to market.

Lots of animals are native to Bangladesh, including the endangered Bengal tiger.

the Netherlands

The capital of the Netherlands, Amsterdam, is a beautiful city filled with lots of plants and miles of canals. People sail up and down the canals on narrow boats—some people sell food and flowers from their boats, and others even live on them.

Amsterdam is full of bikes, with thousands of people cycling the city's streets every day.

The tulip is the national flower of the Netherlands and the cities and countryside can be covered with colorful blooms.

There are lots of cafes on the streets, where people can sit and watch the city go by while enjoying coffee, pastries, and thin, caramel-filled waffles called *stroopwafels*.

About the Illustrator

Greg Paprocki is a prolific artist who is always trying to push the limits of his imagination. His creativity, drive, and careful attention to detail is reflected in his art. And though he is a one-man shop, Greg's polished, inventive work evokes the skills set of an entire team of artists. He's always finding new ways to bring to life the plethora of beautiful ideas inside his head, and has designed many books, games, and characters.

Disclaimer

Weldon Owen take pride in doing their best to get the facts right in putting together the information in this book, but occasionally something slips past their beady eyes. Therefore they make no warranties about the accuracy or completeness of the information in the book and to the maximum extent permitted, disclaim all liability. Wherever possible, any errors of fact will be corrected at reprint.

While Weldon Owen strives for accuracy in all their titles, the examples of people's lives in this book are in no way representative of the lives and experiences of people in an entire country or area. Everyone's life is different, and there is no way to cover the vast diversity of our world in one book.